The Too-Tight Tutu

Merry dreams of being
a true ballerina—wearing a sparkling
tutu and dancing gracefully
across the stage.

No one else seems to believe in her,
and things keep getting in her way.

But Merry is not about
to give up easily.

MORE BITES TO SINK YOUR TEETH INTO!

BIG BAD BUNNIES
Danny Katz
Illustrated by Mitch Vane

CRAZY FOR CAKE!
Phillip Gwynne
Illustrated by Gus Gordon

THE GUTLESS GLADIATOR
Margaret Clark
Illustrated by Terry Denton

LET IT RIP!
Archimede Fusillo
Illustrated by Stephen Michael King

LUKE AND LULU
Bruce Davis
Illustrated by Chantal Stewart

MISS WOLF AND THE PORKERS
Bill Condon
Illustrated by Caroline Magerl

The Too-Tight Tutu

WILL PRACTICE MAKE MERRY PERFECT?

Sherryl Clark

Illustrated by Cathy Wilcox

RUNNING PRESS
KIDS
PHILADELPHIA·LONDON

For Brian, and for Donna,
who deserves a tutu of her own

First published by Penguin Books Australia, 1997

First published in the United States by
Running Press Book Publishers, 2007

Printed in China

9   8   7   6   5   4   3   2   1
Digit on the right indicates the number of this printing

Library of Congress Control Number: 2006929400
ISBN-13: 978-0-7624-3046-8
ISBN-10: 0-7624-3046-X

Original design by Ruth Grüner, Penguin Books Australia
Additional design for this edition by Frances J. Soo Ping Chow

Typography: New Century School Book
This book may be ordered by mail from the publisher.
Please include $2.50 for postage and handling.
But try your bookstore first!

This edition published by Running Press Kids, an imprint of
Running Press Book Publishers
2300 Chestnut Street
Philadelphia, PA 19103-4371

Visit us on the web!
www.runningpress.com

Ages 7–10
Grades 2–4

One

Merry wanted to be a ballerina. In her dreams, she saw herself gliding across a stage in a silver tutu, with lots of sparkly sequins and silver ballet shoes.

But she had three problems.

There was no ballet school in the small country town where she lived.

Even if there had been, her mother said, "We can't afford it. Ballet schools are very expensive."

And Merry thought she was too fat to be a ballerina. Her little brother Sam said so all the time. He also said,

"You're ugly," and "You're dumb," but mostly he said, "You're too fat to be a ballet dancer, Merry."

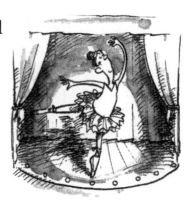

Other people weren't as rude but Merry knew they thought so, too. She was always picked last for T-ball and she always came last in running races. Still, she knew that she could be a ballet dancer if only she had the chance.

One day, a tall, skinny woman came to Merry's school. She said, "I'm a ballet teacher. If enough children are interested, I will teach ballet once a week at the local hall."

All the girls ran home to ask their parents. Finally, eight girls signed up, enough for a class.

On the first day, the teacher stood waiting for them in the old wooden hall. Her long blonde hair was tied up in a bright scarf and big gold rings dangled from her ears.

"Look at her shoes," Merry's friend Susie whispered. "Real ones with points."

Merry stared enviously at the worn pink shoes and the ribbons laced around the teacher's ankles.

"Girls, girls." A loud clap of hands. "My name is Shirley Lane. You can call me Miss Lane or Madame." She stressed the *dame*. "I realize this is your first day but—" Miss Lane pursed her lips at the line-up of T-shirts, shorts, and sneakers in front of her. "You will need black leotards, pink tights, and ballet shoes for class."

Merry's heart rose at the thought of her very own feet in those pink ballet shoes, then it sank into her stomach. She felt sick. Mom had grumbled

4

about the cost of the classes. When she heard about the leotard, tights, and shoes she'd just say no.

But Miss Lane gave them no time to worry about such problems. "Bare feet, girls, off with those clodhoppers. Now, positions of the feet. First position."

Soon they were all using old wooden chairs as barres to balance against. Merry carefully twisted her feet around and back, around and back. Then her arms. Up and down. Rounded nicely. Up and down. Out and up.

"My arms ache," hissed Susie.

"When are we going to dance?"

"No talking, girls," Miss Lane called. "Up, down, third position, that's it."

Finally, they lined up in the middle of the floor and Miss Lane began to show them the first steps of a

dance. Merry counted them, six movements which advanced her forward and back a total of six feet. Suddenly the class was over.

"Practice at home every night, girls. Here's a note about your class dates and where to buy your outfits."

Merry took her letter home and

handed it to her mother, holding her breath, waiting for the expected response.

"Every Wednesday, pay a class in advance. Buy from her aunt's shop," Mom muttered. "That'd be right. Did you like it, Merry?"

"Yes, Mom, it was great." Merry bounced as she talked. "We did first position, second position, third position . . . look, I'll show you."

"I haven't got time now, wait until after dinner," Mom said. She went to fetch potatoes from the laundry room . Merry waited until she returned.

"Mom?"

"Yes?"

"What about the leotard and tights and shoes?"

"You'll have to do without the tights, I'm afraid. I've got you a leotard from the church shop and some pink slip-ons. You'll have to sew the ribbons on yourself. They're in your room."

Merry's mouth dropped open then she raced into her bedroom. There on her bed lay a real black leotard like Miss Lane's and a small plastic packet. She pulled off her T-shirt and shorts and stepped into the leotard, sliding it up slowly. It fitted everywhere except the arms and shoulders.

Mom stood in the doorway. "I'll shorten the sleeves and put a couple of tucks in the shoulders. What about the shoes?"

Merry slid them out of the packet and tried to swallow her disappointment. They sort of looked like ballet shoes. "They'll be fine when you sew the ribbons on," said Mom.

Merry just nodded. To her the shoes looked like her nana's slippers and she hated them.

Two

At the ballet class next week Merry tried not to look at the other girls in their brand new leotards, pink tights, and real ballet shoes. Even Susie had proper shoes, pale pink and fitted, not old-lady pink and elasticized around the tops. Merry decided to make up for her bare legs and funny shoes by dancing and practicing three times as hard as everyone else. No, ten times as hard.

She tried to ignore Sam, who sat on the steps and laughed every time she wobbled.

"You'll never do it. You're too fat," he giggled.

"Go away, Sam," she said. "You're being a big pain."

"Teach me to dance, Merry. I want to be a dancing elephant too."

"Mom!" yelled Merry, and Mom came out to drag Sam away.

Sometimes Merry looked down at her roly-poly body as she practiced, but really that was the least of her worries.

She just couldn't seem to follow the dance steps. Once Merry was on the floor, it was as if she forgot which was left and which was right, which was third position, where her arms should go. If she got her feet right, her arms were like limp asparagus. In her dreams she danced right off the stage into the wings, forgetting when to stop.

But finally, her nightly practice began to work. What previously had to be counted, step by step, move by move, gradually became second nature. At last the basics stuck in her brain so she could move on to the harder steps and combinations.

Finally, Miss Lane began to smile at her and say, "Good girl, Merry, that's the way," instead of, "No, Merry, try it again."

All too soon it was school break and ballet class was over for that term. Miss Lane made a special announcement on the last day.

"When we return next term, we

shall start working on a group piece. The annual Silver Slippers Competitions are coming up soon and I'd like to enter you. Anyone who would like to try a solo, see me after the break. That's all girls."

Merry's eyes lit up and she ran all the way home. When she burst into the kitchen, she was so puffed and red in the face that her mother made her sit down and put a wet cloth on her face. Merry pushed it away. She'd got her breath back enough to talk.

"We're going in the competitions, Mom. In the city. Miss Lane said I can do a solo. I'll get to wear a real tutu."

"Really?" Mom frowned. She already knew Miss Lane's aunt owned a dancers' costume hire shop. Miss Lane had recommended it. It was in the big town twenty-five miles away and it was expensive.

"And we're going to perform a group dance too. I can't wait." Merry twirled around the kitchen, so excited she couldn't sit still.

"Hmmm," said Mom, and went back to getting dinner ready. Wednesday night was sausages night.

All through the long break—really only two weeks but it seemed like forever—Merry danced. She practiced

on the back porch then danced her
own compositions on the lawn. She
circled the lemon tree, whirled past
the vegetables, and stepped around
another tree. Outside on the grass
she felt light and floaty. So different
to the old wooden hall, where her feet
thumped and echoed on the floor.

At last, it was time for a new term of classes. Merry arrived early and as soon as Miss Lane got out of her car, Merry said, "I want to do a solo, Miss Lane, by myself, with a tutu."

Miss Lane pursed her lips. "I'm not sure about that, Merry. It's a big thing to dance on your own, learn steps by yourself with no one else to follow."

"I can do it, Miss Lane. Please let me."

Miss Lane just shook her head and said, "I'll think about it. Maybe I'll give you something small to see how you do. But I'm not promising."

That was enough for Merry. She

knew she could dance by herself.
All she needed was the chance. And
the tutu.

Miss Lane clapped her hands and
all the girls lined up. "Warm ups,
girls, some revision of what we
learned last term. Then we'll start on
our group piece."

This was serious. Miss Lane had
brought real music, with violins and
flutes playing, and she had worked
out a dance which involved all the
girls at once. They ran in from each
corner, met in the middle, circled, and
stepped. It was lucky there were eight
of them. The steps seemed awfully

difficult compared with the ones they'd done before.

"We'd have to learn a dance with more steps and combinations," said Miss Lane. "It's a competition. You'll have to do lots of practice at home."

Merry was used to that but she saw some of the girls making faces. Tennis season and the T-ball competition were starting. They didn't want to give those up to practice boring old ballet.

The next week was the same, and the week after. No one could get the steps right, in the right order, all together. Miss Lane pursed her lips more and more and Merry could see that very soon the competition idea would be dropped. And maybe Miss Lane would stop her classes too.

After all her efforts, Merry could see her dream slowly slipping away again. She gritted her teeth and clenched her fists. Miss Lane *had* to give them another chance. Merry devised a plan.

Three

That afternoon after class Merry called the other girls together outside the hall.

"You have to practice more," she pleaded. "Miss Lane won't let us enter if you don't."

"So?" said Belinda, who was last year's under

12 tennis champion. "I don't have time." She swung her strong, tanned arms, pretending to hit a tennis ball.

"And it's boring," said Sally. "Same old thing over and over."

"Don't you want to wear a tutu?" Merry said.

"I suppose," said Sally.

Merry had a brainwave.

"If you all come to my house on Saturday and practice, I'll get Mom to make us her super chocolate cake. You can eat the whole cake."

Merry's mom made the best chocolate cake in town. All the girls' mouths watered and they finally agreed. Merry walked slowly home, wondering how she could possibly persuade her mother to make a cake so eight girls could dance on their back lawn. She guessed the best way was just to ask.

To her surprise, Mom said, "All right, Merry, just this once. I can see it's important to you."

The next day at school, Merry told all the girls to come at ten o'clock. That way they'd be fresh and not rushing off to other things.

"Are you sure we're getting a whole cake?" Belinda asked, suspiciously.

"Yes," Mom said. "And Dad's going to mow the lawn specially."

Merry's dad was a truck driver and he mowed lawns faster and neater than anyone else on the street.

"What about that gross brother of yours?" said Sally. "He'd better not be watching."

"Dad's taking him fishing," said Merry.

Saturday came and all the girls turned up. Merry was nervous but determined. They *had* to learn the dance. She made them repeat the steps over and over.

"You're too bossy," whined Sally.

"Just shut up and do it," snapped Belinda, "then we can go."

After an hour, Merry thought they finally had it right. She brought out the cake and cut it into eight huge slices. Seven girls stuffed it into their mouths. "Your mother makes the best cake ever," mumbled Susie.

"You can have my piece later," whispered Merry. Susie was a real

friend. She was the only one who hadn't complained but had just kept practicing.

The next Wednesday Miss Lane put on the music and watched, lips tight, expecting the usual shambles. Except for a couple of steps in the middle where Merry stood on Sally's foot,

they danced it exactly right. Miss
Lane beamed.

"That's excellent, girls. See what
practice can do? I'm very pleased."

After class, Merry approached Miss Lane. "Can I do my solo now?" she asked.

"I don't think so, Merry," Miss Lane said. "We won't have time for you to practice it properly, the group has taken so long."

Susie was standing behind Merry. "She can do it, Miss Lane. It was Merry who made everyone practice and get it right. She practices more than all of us put together."

"Is that so?" Miss Lane stared at Merry for several long moments. "All right, Merry. I'll start you off on the first part and if you manage to learn that by next week, you can do the whole solo."

By the third week, adding a few more movements at each class, even Miss Lane had to admit that Merry could do it.

At home, Mom frowned at Merry's hours on the back porch. "Have you done your homework? Set the table? Is your room tidy?" But Merry had finished all those tasks at super high speed so she could practice.

Soon her slip-ons had worn out. Mom tried to stitch them up but even she couldn't fix the big holes worn in the soles.

Miss Lane noticed the very next week. "You can't dance in those, anyway," she said. "You need proper shoes." She had also noticed long ago the second-hand leotard and bare legs. "I might have an old pair somewhere you can have. I'll look."

That week Merry practiced in bare feet. Her slip-ons fell apart. "Miss Lane is finding me an old pair of hers, Mom. They won't cost much. Lucky I've got big feet."

Mom just smiled. "That's all right, Merry. I'm sure we could stretch to another pair of shoes if we have to."

The shoes Miss Lane brought in were faded and had no ribbons, and they were a little too big, so Merry had to wear two pairs of socks. But they were real ballet shoes, not slip-ons. At last, Merry felt she was getting close to being a ballerina.

The solo dance she learned used nearly the whole floor space. Miss Lane said, "The stage in the competition theater is as big as this hall. Imagine that wall there is the front of the stage. That way, you'll know where the judges and the audience are. You should face them all the time."

Judges? Audience? Suddenly the

competition was becoming real.
The other girls twittered over their
costumes, pale blue floating chiffon
dresses. All the mothers were given
another letter about the cost of the
material and how to make it into
a dress.

Mom hmphed. "I suppose I could
use it for curtains later," she said.

Merry waited for Miss Lane to
mention her tutu. At last, she could
wait no longer and asked, "Will I get
to wear a tutu, Miss Lane?"

"Well . . ." Miss Lane hesitated. "I
was going to say you could wear the
blue dress in your solo as well."

Four

Merry's face fell, and she felt tears burning in her eyes, threatening to spill out. Miss Lane bent close and patted Merry's shoulder.

"All right, Merry, since you've worked so hard I'll see if there's something I can borrow from my aunt. We'll need to measure you first." She pulled a large tape measure from her bag. "Hmmm, you're a big girl, aren't you?"

Merry looked down at herself. The roly-poly body was still there. All this time, she'd felt light and graceful.

She'd forgotten she was so round
and heavy.

"I really don't think Aunt Helen
will have anything to fit you. Don't get
your hopes up."

For a whole week Merry felt sick.
All that hard work and no tutu. It
wasn't fair.

Mom said, "What's wrong, Merry? Surely you've learned your dance perfectly by now?"

"Yes, Mom."

"So why the long face?"

"Miss Lane said she won't be able to find a tutu to fit me. Why am I so fat?" she cried.

"You're not fat, love. You're a good healthy eater. You'll slim down naturally when you get older, just like I did. In the meantime, a few less cookies and candy might help."

Merry felt like starving herself but she knew that wouldn't work in a week. Besides, she got too hungry.

Wednesday arrived and there were only two weeks until the competition. All of the girls brought their dresses with them to try on, they even practiced in them. That cheered Miss Lane up immensely. "Lovely, girls, just lovely." But she never mentioned the tutu.

Another letter to take home. It gave the address of the theater and what time to be there. Merry had two times on her page. "You'll all need stage make-up," Miss Lane said. "Your mothers can help you put it on. Don't forget to bring your dresses and we'll use the changing rooms behind the stage. Please don't be late."

Now that the day was so close, everyone was excited and happy to practice the dance over and over. Merry performed her solo at the end of the class. Only Susie stayed to watch.

"How did I look, Susie?" Merry asked. All she could hear was her feet thumping across the floor like a hippopotamus.

"Fantastic," said Susie. "I wish I'd done a solo."

Miss Lane clapped her hands. "Now Merry, your dance is fine. You're not nervous, are you?" Merry shook her head. "Good. Now, the tutu. I have two possibilities but if they're not suitable, the blue dress will have to do."

Merry nodded, her heart beating like a bass drum. Miss Lane opened a suitcase she'd carried in from her car. Two bundles of lace and net unfolded like sparkling butterflies. One was white and red with red

roses across the skirt, the other was pale pink and silver, with glittering snowflakes sewn onto the front.

"They might not fit," Miss Lane warned. She held out the white and red tutu first. Merry pulled it up over her leotard but even she could see right away that the zipper was a few inches away from meeting. She stepped out of that tutu and turned to the pink and silver one. It was almost too much to hope for. She pulled it up slowly and looped the straps over her shoulders.

"Those aren't straps, Merry, they're just to hang it up by. Now, how does this one fit? Pull your tummy in."

Merry sucked in her breath and held it. Behind her she heard the zipper slide up.

"It's a bit tight," Miss Lane said. "And it sags at the bottom. And the top of the bodice is a bit high."

She frowned and Merry pleaded. "It's fine, really. Mom can tack the bottom up. I can breathe okay. It fits just right."

Miss Lane sighed. "All right, Merry. I suppose it's passable. But you must take good care of it. And your mother must hand stitch, not use the machine."

"Yes, Miss Lane. I'll tell her."

Merry reluctantly pulled the tutu down and stepped out of it. She'd barely had time to think about how it felt. Miss Lane carefully folded the tutu over again and placed it on a hanger with a plastic cover.

"Can you carry it home without damaging it?" she asked.

"Yes, Miss Lane. I'll be very, very careful."

"Hmmm," was the reply. "I'd better give you a lift."

So Merry arrived home with an armful of pink and silver net and lace, sitting bolt upright in the passenger seat of Miss Lane's car. Mom came out to say hello, and Miss Lane passed the tutu to her.

"It's really a little too tight," Miss Lane said. "Don't let Merry grow any in the next two weeks or she'll have to wear the blue dress."

"No problems," said Mom, smiling at Merry. "I'm sure she'll fit it just fine. And I'll stitch the bottom up with a few tucks."

"Fine. I'll see you at the theater then. Goodbye."

Miss Lane drove off in a cloud of dust and Mom held the tutu up in front of her.

"It's beautiful, isn't it? You'll look

like a real ballerina in this."

Mom couldn't have said anything better. Merry was so happy and excited she thought she might explode.

"Can I try it on again now, Mom? Please?"

"I suppose so. Then I can see where it has to be altered."

Merry was inside in a couple of seconds, into her bedroom and yanking other clothes off. Mom followed behind, carrying the tutu and then sliding it out of its cover. Merry stepped into it and slid it up her body. The lace and sparkling strips were prickly where the seams met on the inside, but that didn't matter. Merry turned slowly and looked at herself in the mirror. Her face crumpled.

"I don't look like a ballerina at all!" she wailed.

Five

"Don't be silly," Mom said sharply. "Wait until you have make-up on, and your hair in a little bun, and your shoes on. Then you'll see."

But Merry wasn't convinced. Somehow, she'd expected to turn and see a wonderful transformation in the mirror. No more roly-poly Merry with long stringy hair, short legs, and round face. Instead, a tall, graceful, beautiful ballerina should have been smiling back at her.

Mom pinned up the bottom of the bodysuit part where it sagged and tried to pull the bodice down a bit, but it wouldn't budge. "You'll have to remember what Miss Lane said. No over-eating or this won't fit at all. I'll have to reinforce the stitching around the zipper as it is."

"Yeah, all right," Merry muttered.

She took off the tutu and let Mom take it away to her sewing corner without a protest. She thought about going out on the back porch and practicing, but somehow she couldn't raise the energy. Instead, she wandered into the living room and turned on the TV.

She sat and watched all evening without saying a word. She didn't hear

Sam arguing with Dad about who caught the biggest fish, or everyone laughing at the comedian with the broken glasses. Mom looked as if she was about to say something to Merry once or twice, but didn't.

At next week's class, the last before the competition, everyone performed the dance perfectly. Merry felt as if her feet weighed a hundred pounds each, she could barely move them. But she didn't make any mistakes, not even in her solo, so Miss Lane said nothing.

At the end of the class, she said, "See you all at the theater, girls. Don't be late." Then she was gone.

The day of the competition soon arrived. Merry felt so dejected. Her feet were still heavy and she hadn't practiced all week. She just wanted the day to be over. Mom came in as she was packing her little bag with shoes, a pair of Mom's pantyhose, a hairbrush, and hairpins.

"Are you ready?" Mom asked. "Dad's got the car waiting."

"Dad's coming?" Merry said. "What for?"

"We're all coming to watch you, even Sam," said Mom. "We want to see you dance, of course."

"Sam's coming?" Merry yelled. "No, he can't, he has to stay home. He'll ruin it. He'll make it even worse!"

"Don't be silly! He won't be anywhere near you, he'll be in the audience. Come on, we'll be late."

Merry trailed out behind her mother and got into the backseat of the car, hunching up and sitting as far away from Sam as possible. In between them lay the tutu, shining and silvery in the sunlight.

"Miss Piggy was a ballerina," Sam whispered, but Merry glared at him so angrily that he shut up right away and looked out the window instead.

They arrived at the theater in plenty of time and Mom and Merry walked around to the stage door, leaving Dad and Sam to find their seats. In the dressing room, girls of all ages sat and stood in every available space, and their tutus were every color of the rainbow. Merry stared at them enviously. Not one of them was fat. They were all as thin as poles and looked like the real thing. Merry didn't want to even put her tutu on. She knew they'd all laugh at her. Suddenly, Miss Lane appeared in the doorway.

"We're in the next room," she said. "Come along. Your group dance is in forty minutes and you haven't got make-up on yet."

Merry and Mom followed her into the next room where the other seven girls were already in their floaty blue dresses. Their mothers were all there too, smoothing on make-up, coloring eyelids, and painting on lipstick. Merry and Mom found a spare corner and began getting ready. Mom worked quickly and soon Merry's face was covered in the required make-up. Her hair was drawn up into a bun on top of her head and blue flowers were threaded through it. She pulled on the blue dress and bent to tie her shoe ribbons. Then she headed for the door with the rest of the girls.

"Don't you want to look at yourself in the mirror?" Mom asked.

Merry just shook her head and followed Susie towards the stage stairs.

Miss Lane beckoned to Mom. "You can watch from the front if you're quick. Go through the side door."

Merry stood in the wings, silent

among seven whispering girls. Susie nudged her. "Are you nervous? I'm so scared, I think I'm going to wet myself." Merry just shrugged. "What's the matter? Cheer up."

Belinda turned around and hissed, "Get it together, Merry. If you mess this up for us, I'll strangle you!" Merry nodded and tried to feel more enthusiastic. She heard the familiar music start and suddenly they were all running onto the stage. The lights were incredibly bright. She couldn't see beyond the edge of the stage and had no idea how many people were there.

This is it! she thought.

Six

The shock spurred her on to dance,
the missing energy surging back along
her arms and legs. She knew it by
heart and put her whole body into it.
Susie grinned at her as they passed in
a sequence of steps, and even Belinda
smiled as she circled her in the last
movement.

All too soon it was over and they
were running off again. Merry dimly
heard some clapping, then Miss Lane
was there, shepherding them back to
the dressing room. The other girls
chattered excitedly and Miss Lane

had to hush them.

"Now Merry, you have half an hour before you're on again. Your mother will be back to help you in a minute. Here she is."

Mom entered, her face flushed and her eyes bright. "That was wonderful, girls," she said. "You looked so pretty, like dancing fairies."

"They did very well," Miss Lane agreed. "Merry is on at 2:30. She needs a little more eye make-up, I think. Try this sparkly blue."

Mom set to work on Merry's face again and renewed her lipstick. Then the pink and sliver tutu was revealed in all its magnificence. Mom helped to slide it on and do up the zipper. "It's a little looser," she said. "You must have lost a pound or two." Merry had been so depressed for the past two weeks, she hadn't eaten anything apart from the meals Mom had put in front of her. At least something good had happened.

"Now," Mom said, "turn around and look at yourself."

Merry sighed. Did she have to? She turned and gasped. "I look . . . I look . . . is that me?"

"Certainly is." Mom laughed. "I told you the whole costume with everything added would look different."

Merry gazed at herself in wonder.
Yes, she was still roly-poly but she
looked like a real ballerina from top to
toes. Mom drew a box from her

handbag. "Here," she said. "This is from me and your dad."

Merry opened the box and shrieked. "A tiara!"

"Let's get those flowers out of your hair and pin it on," Mom said. "You'll look just like a fairy."

But Merry didn't want to look like a fairy. She had wished for so long to look like a real ballerina and now it was coming true. The tiara sat in front of her bun and glittered like a row of diamonds.

"Time to go," Mom said. "Let me take a photo first." The flash burst in front of Merry's eyes and she blinked.

In just a few seconds she was out of the dressing room and waiting in the wings, again. As she stood alone, listening for the opening bars of music, Merry felt as if she was in a dream. The kind where she was as light as a feather, drifting along on the breeze. The music began and she stepped out onto the stage. There was no one else there but her. One single spotlight found her and she was bathed in a large pool of light.

Merry thought, how will the light man know where I am going to dance? But it was too late to worry. The dance began and she glided across the

huge expanse. It was as if Merry was dancing only for herself. She couldn't see or hear anyone else. It was like being on her back lawn at home. "There's the lemon tree," she told herself, "and the veggie garden." And Merry turned and skipped and stepped, and her arms dipped and rose. She knew she was dancing perfectly, maybe not like a prima ballerina, but she gave it every ounce of dancing grace that she had inside her.

Then it was over. Merry curtsied low to the judges, just as Miss Lane had taught her, and heard the clapping again. Then she heard a boy's voice,

yelling across the auditorium. "Way to go, Merry!" It was Sam. She laughed and ran off the stage to where Miss Lane waited near the stairs.

"That was very good, Merry. I didn't know you had it in you. We'll make a ballet dancer out of you yet."

But Merry knew she was already a dancer. She knew it inside where it counted. When the points were announced at the end of her section and she hadn't even come third, it didn't matter a bit. She had worn a real tutu and danced on a real stage and most of all, she'd looked like a real ballerina. That was what mattered.

From Sherryl Clark

Merry's story came from remembering when I tried to be a ballerina once, for a whole year. I have a picture in my head of the old hall, the wooden chairs we used as barres, and of us thumping around, trying to learn steps and positions. My tutu was black and red, but it was as tight as Merry's!

From Cathy Wilcox

I grew up in Sydney and, as a roly-poly seven year old, aspired to being a graceful ballerina. My solo performance in front of the class was voted by all to be the most ordinary, and after a year, with no tutu in sight, I gave up. I'm over it now.